I know I am but summer to your heart,

And not the full four seasons of the year.

- Edna St. Vincent Millay

D1664774

the unrequited lover comes back after years of silence
And in the kitchen, you weep. Scrub syrup from plates

& pour curdling wine into the gullet of the sink drain.

Wait for him to admit it wasn't just sex.

That he's been dying the whole time he was gone

to see you again,

not just your bed.

And you sit with clenched fists

on the subway, trying to remember

the shape of someone's hands

when they aren't busy hurting you.

When they aren't using you.

And he kisses you like he's forgotten

the name of the ocean, when really

the only name he's forgotten is yours.

reincarnation

someday, we meet in another life.

on another star.

we forget for a while

how everything is doomed.

how you'll go back to her

after this,

how you'd hang the sun in the sky

if she asked.

they say the most beautiful stars

have the ugliest endings.

alone on valentine's day

Plato once wrote that every human

has a soulmate,

another half, a pursuit of wholeness.

who ever said that other half

couldn't be you?

that the worst parts of you

would one day meet the best?

Traitor

they say Anne Boleyn had an extra finger,

that she hid it beneath velvet robes

and gloves of lace.

all your extra parts, all your extra love,

is nothing to hide.

nothing to bandage or bundle.

they say Anne finally revealed her finger

with her head on the block

as the scythe came down.

don't wait until the very end

to love yourself.

arithmetic

i would have given you everything.

even myself,

with no questions asked.

that's when i knew it was time

to end things.

i am the answer.

i am my own answer.

How to Play Dead

1. Crack open like a dictionary in the arms of everyone who promises to love you like you were meant to be. Close in the face of everyone who kept their hands over your mouth, in the face of whiskey, in the face of mean girls in dark lipstick who cry when they're drunk about their absent fathers then kick you when you're down, when they're sober.

2. Don't go back to that boy again. The one made of motor oil and salt, the one who can do everything with his tongue but nothing with his heart. The one who hands you the poisoned apple and then expects you to kiss his fingers.

3. Relearn how to bellow in your sleep, how to split the sky with your loudness, with the howling cry for milk you were born with. It's only when the men come that we long to crawl back into the womb. Don't forget to thank your mother.

4. Be bruja. Be bruja. Be bruja. Forget how easy flirting with death is and ask life for a dance. Season the sorrow inside you until it comes to a boil. It will always feed you well.

5. Everything will be beautiful again.

drinking about you

the best parts of blacking out

were always the ones

where i forgot

how you didn't love me.

hook, line, and sinker

they lost many fish that month.

they washed ashore in droves, scales

falling like glitter into the sand.

bellies swollen into globes.

there was nothing much

left to eat. only what they could scavenge.

when the time came,

they cut them open, fins and all.

inside each one was a wedding ring.

the wives left that day.

on their way to find new lives,

like salmon swimming upstream.

the bartender of broken hearts

stop trying to fill yourself. you were never empty. drink, raid the medicine cabinet, weep and moan and cast spells on every man who wronged you, but my god, don't you dare consider yourself empty. the moon may have craters but it still spills out moonlight.

and, my god, the only time you should ever empty yourself for another is at birth.

not after. not in-between. not ever again.

Chimera

Everything your mother has ever cooked

blooms in the oven like a violet.

Griddle steeped in grease,

chicken simmering

in its own fat.

Apricots opening into flared bowls,

set like jewels in folds of dough.

Every man you've ever loved

drinks a screwdriver in the living room.

Your mother is kissing each one with tongue,

houses extinguishing light across the street,

until each man sinks like a doll to the floor,

ready & waiting

to fall through the cellar door.

I Want You

I want your hunchbacked soul, I want to plant a thousand emerald lilies between your thighs and bring you coffee in the shower then drop the mug on the stall floor and cut our feet on the pieces, drop the mug and kiss you instead, tongue into tongue, moving together like fish, I want to translate the moving dips of moon across your spine at night when loneliness is so real even when we're together, I want to tuck my feet into the backs of your knees for warmth, I want your messy crying and your messy nights with you begging to be buried six feet under, want to rub your back when the endless heaves of too much wine bends you over the toilet, I want to hurt you and save you and love you then do it all again, I want to lap up your apologies like milk, to watch your face as you come, to see you above me stretching and arcing, to be the animal that lives inside you, the last one to see you alive, I want the needle and the shot going into your blood, I want this prairie in your mind, I want to hold you howling at a funeral and see you birthed again, want us to pick bones clean of their meat and feed the remains to the birds, to find the mouse that choked to death on a bottle cap and lower it into the soil with you singing some dirge in your soft voice, I want the day we finally decide not to use the condoms, the teeth growing back, autumn you fell back in love with your body, the summer you'll fall out of love with me, the winter you'll plummet into it again, the terrible, miserable, wrenching things we'll say and do to each other, I want to count crows and arrows and sunsets, for you to look at me like a crown, to grow back into and out of your arms, I want the proposal, I want you to be here on the nights when my past undoes me, for you to push inside me and hold my face between your hands, to be sweaty with you, I want all your I hurt you and sorry and love and I won't do it again's, your thighs in the shower, your mouth in my hair, your toothbrush finally next to mine in the bathroom glass, I want us to dig out of our own graves and crawl into each other's with roses in our mouths.

Last Supper

The neighbors, for years, would invite the dead.

Would invite their lost lovers.

Venison laid open in honey on the table,

risotto crackling in its tureen.

Grape leaves so full with salt they sunk

into each guest's palms.

They dragged them from the river,

from backyard pools,

drunks from alleyways

with bottles still in their hands.

Like a feast could bring them back.

Like their mouths could be full of anything

but water or smoke.

As if the daughter they lost

could ever be seated again

with a plate before her body.

please don't get back with her

i think

i got lost in you so deeply

i forgot my way out.

dating rituals for lovers who hate each other

black widows devour their mates

after courtship.

female praying mantises

bite the heads

off their partners.

the paper nautilus octopus

releases part of itself to the female

before swimming away

to die quietly.

in my dreams, one of us

is always hungry.

one of us

will always ruin the other.

but we can't stop long enough

to watch it happen.

The Men I've Fucked

He used to dip birds in gasoline and strike a match.

Later, graduated to squirrels and then cats,

strays from an alleyway

or pressed against the sides of bars.

For weeks afterward,

I smelled like something rotting.

All along the edge of my house,

fir trees deep as silver.

Touch one needle,

and the rest would fall.

Back then

it wasn't called what it is now.

We were supposed to be grateful

they even looked at us.

sorrow as riddle

grief is messy.

so is unloving.

sometimes, they leave us

with blood on our hands

and blood in our mouths.

and sometimes, they leave us

wiping blood on each other.

forgetting a name

Curl it around your tongue,

taste it, breathe in

the darkness of it, the black cherry,

the sour rotted salt.

say it over and over again,

until you almost forget your own.

and when the time comes,

forget the person attached to it.

10 Ways I Know He Doesn't Love Me Anymore

1. Our bedroom drawers are filled with doorknobs he has never gotten around to installing. All around the house, doors stand empty of their most necessary parts. He comes and goes so often he has no need for fixing the things that separate us- what are doors, when we already have these walls we've built up between ourselves.

2. There is lipstick stained into the edges of coffee cups I've never touched.

3. The few nights we sleep together, he handles me like you might handle someone recently passed away: fondly, with respect, but already planning for the life ahead without them.

4. In one photo of my parents, my father's face is obscured by a giant sunflower, its heavy body curled around his shoulders in gold like the outlines of an eclipse. In the next photo, it is my mother's, hidden by a rose that matches the color I imagine her mouth to be.

5. He's taken to eating handfuls of fruit every night before drinking, peaches round as river stones, pears flushed with pink, blackberries so dark their purple globes rim his fingertips like they've been slammed in the car door. He wants something to sink his teeth into, but has to settle for me.

6. We don't speak in terms of the future anymore, only the past. We don't sleep together. We slept together. It makes sense, then, why he only remembers to kiss me when he's already on the way to work.

7. The hallway mirror next to the shadowbox never captures both our faces anymore- always him alone, or me standing by myself. Either I'm a vampire, or he's a ghost. And every fantasy writer knows the two aren't compatible.

8. The moon was never full on any of our anniversaries, always gibbous or crescent.

9. Neither of us sleepwalks, as far as I can tell, but lately I've been hearing someone pacing in the kitchen and moving out onto the patio late at night, steps emptying into darkness like stones skipped across the surface of a pond. Sometimes I hear two pairs of steps, hoping it's the wind and not some other woman.

10. An old Cherokee legend tells of a grandfather who reveals to his grandson how evil and good are always fighting inside of him like two wolves. When asked which wolf wins the fight, the grandfather replies, "The one I feed." I know he has been feeding his desire to leave. I know I am nothing but kindling for this, just stoking the fire.

Ad Hominem

They uncover thirteen skulls and seven jawbones

from his house years later

the grass growing like spears in the front yard.

How close we were to going under

not just the bills & payments

but beneath the earth,

two birds turning south

instead of east

his fingers patting down the dirt

over our heads

like seed.

In summer he grew magnolia trees

with blooms the size of human heads;

looking back

we'd always insist

we should have known.

poet's lament

i could have loved you

better than anyone else

if only you had let me.

Black Dahlia

Mother, it was the forest that drove him mad.

We feasted on spinach and baked potatoes sunk in butter,

their skins opening like envelopes,

and there was Merlot for days,

a handful of sunflower seeds to quell the taste.

He unfastened the birches from their white papers

one by one, until only the bones were left,

scattered the remains to the wind like ashes,

and took me down into that hollow, Mother,

that hollow beneath the fallen tree,

where moss grew & softened into leaves,

and it was there

that he got to work.

When he was done, my palms were puppet limbs

and Mother, my body,

my body was none.

leaving and loving are not the same thing. leaving and loving are not the same thing.

sick leave

in this universe, you do not get out of bed

for weeks. let the dishes pile

like porcelain castles in the sink,

leave your hair unwashed,

its oiled red staining the sheets.

the dogs down the street

wag their tongues with disapproval

instead of their tails.

it is so much easier to be understood

when grief is the kind

that comes from death.

but the kind that comes

from someone not loving you back

is sharper, fiercer somehow.

less able to be forgiven.

everyone else seems to think

you are just playing dead.

amour perdu

in my dreams,

you leave dark knots of your hair

in my backyard like black pearls.

when fed with water,

they bloom into inky roses.

you wake me up from one dream

into another with your mouth

between my legs.

we swim into the deep end

of each other, til we sink,

til our pulses introduce one another.

inside my bed, you place

a thousand love letters,

one for every day you've loved me.

but when i open my eyes,

the only letters i still remember

are the ones i shouted

when i was calling your name

to come back.

prayers for unrequited atheists

In *Genesis,* Noah expects the ark to save him. The
animals, too.

In the middle of a flood, no one else can save you but
yourself.

No one else can hold the shutters closed when the entire
house threatens to collapse.

No one else remembers how it feels to drown in the middle
of a flood

while everyone else is swimming.

i wasn't enough. i wasn't enough. i wasn't enough. i
wasn't enough. i wasn't enough. i wasn't enough. i
wasn't enough. i wasn't enough. i wasn't enough. i
wasn't enough. i wasn't enough. i wasn't enough. i
wasn't enough. i wasn't enough. i wasn't enough. i
wasn't enough. i wasn't enough. i wasn't enough. i
wasn't enough. i wasn't enough. i wasn't enough. i
wasn't enough. i wasn't enough. i wasn't enough. i
wasn't enough. i wasn't enough. i wasn't enough. i
wasn't enough. i wasn't enough. i wasn't enough.
i wasn't (more than) enough.

The Pied Piper's Testimony

Your Honor, the bills had not been paid.

The dinner plates left unwashed,

her hair rank across the pillow like aged wine,

each day the light leaving her body

twice as fast as the evening before.

Anyone would do what I have done.

The children were eager for it, notes falling

from my mouth like coins.

It was all for her.

Maybe it was wrong to lead them away

for ransom, to dream of their mothers'

anguished faces, their midnight sorrows.

But here she is, Your Honor, next to me

on the stand, no more light leaving,

all her love

finally paid for.

romeo and juliet, act one, scene never

i've never hurt anyone as much as you.

i've never loved anyone as much either.

Feral

They say that a child thrown to the wolves

will grow up as one.

Will learn how to hunt & prowl

like a predator,

scavenge for human scent.

They say everything is better

in the morning.

I think this thing sucked the life

out of me.

I think you used to be

something gentle.

Something soft and forgiving.

I think you used to know

what love was.

Missed Connections with Lonely Boys

on the train you said the moon is one of those people
who's always late to parties no matter who they're thrown
by. i said parties are so brutal the way the loneliness of
mixed drinks makes us hate one another, then sleep with
everyone we hate until we hate ourselves. you asked if i
wanted to get out of here; i said if by *here* you mean this
life then a thousand times yes. you wanted to go swimming
in a river where the fish grew thick along the banks like
silver glitter. i said my last missed connection gutted me
like a fish too, sliced so deep my belly called it love before
my belly lost our child. too many 3am's sitting in my
underwear on a rooftop with spoiled orange juice. you said
love is a synonym for damage. i said our bodies are a
synonym for light. you told me, this isn't sex. and i said i
know, it's whatever's left.

Desdemona

why do you look at the moon

like it's going to save you?

honey, no one saves someone

they can't even see.

loss

i wish i had asked you

to remember me.

truth is, i know

i'm the first one

you'll forget.

intimate

this thing is a monster.

it haunts, gnashes, weeps,

gnaws. it longs for my bones

like a moth to the light.

it starves whenever

i don't think of you.

it feasts when i do.

just because you never loved me doesn't mean i can't love myself. just because you never loved me doesn't mean i can't love myself. just because you never loved me doesn't mean i can't love myself. just because you never loved me doesn't mean i can't love myself. just because you never loved me doesn't mean i can't love myself. just because you never loved me doesn't mean i can't love myself. just because you never loved me doesn't mean i can't love myself. just because you never loved me doesn't mean i can't love myself. just because you never loved me doesn't mean i can't love myself. just because you never loved me doesn't mean i can't love myself. just because you never loved me doesn't mean i can't love myself. just because you never loved me doesn't mean i can't love myself. *you never loved me*

Pendle Hill

During the Lancashire witch trials,

the witches sent to be hanged

or destroyed with fire

went to their deaths

with their husbands' names in their mouths.

Their throats turned ruby,

limbs went gold & burnished

but their last thoughts

were about the men they loved.

I think I know how this feels.

To lose sleep over something

that I'll never have again.

To know that I could go to the gallows

and all I would see before me

would be you.

on the awfulness of unrequited love

Unrequited love is exhausting, almost physically draining, like teetering on the edge of recovery after being home sick for two weeks. But the problem with unrequited love is that there's no cure, no chicken soup or bedrest to make you feel better again. The heart is a fickle organ, the most unpredictable in the body, and it wants what it wants for sometimes unknowable reasons.

Imagine what it must have been like for Adam and Eve, the first man and woman, just trying out their hearts for the first time. No instruction manual, no step-by-step rules that laid out the foundation and the uses. And if Adam didn't love Eve, or vice versa, there would be no one else to project that unused love onto, no placebo.

When you see the one you love with someone else, it's all you can do not to rip your heart out and throw it on the floor and declare your love to the whole world, to smash every plate in the cupboard or paint the walls with their name. It's gut-wrenching, like asking for the whole universe and only receiving the stars instead.

And of course, if your love is unrequited, you sincerely believe that this person belongs to you, that they are *yours*. That you love them quite possibly more than it is possible to love someone. It's like a Matryoshka doll: you can fit so much feeling inside your own body, again and again, layers upon layers going down, down, into the deepest parts of yourself. If someone were to unpeel you like an onion, they'd find all that unreturned love built up like great yellow reams of fat, insulating your kidneys and lungs, clogging your arteries. You'd never be able to escape it.

Sometimes you lie awake at night in bed and imagine all the things you could have said or done or been, the things that might have changed the course of fate and steered the ship of destiny in your direction for once. But unfortunately, while we have all the maps in the world for faraway countries or oceans or mammoth caves, no one, in the entire course of human history, has ever charted a path for unrequited love and how to find your way out of its forest. The first explorer that does so, and quite possibly the only, would most likely have an entire continent named after them, an entire island, an entire universe. Because the one person who figures out how to escape unrequited love's grasp is truly a genius.

And sometimes you look at their picture over and over again in your school's yearbook, flipping the pages but always returning to that one face, the smile you believe is meant for you, the hair parted just so, the smooth curve of their neck where it joins their collarbones.

You'd write their name upon the stars if you could, but for now you'll just have to settle for jotting it down in your tattered notebook instead.

how to stay when you know he only wants you for the sex

don't.

the worst nightmare

the whole time you had my body,

your mind

was on her.

the whole time you were looking

into my eyes,

you were picturing hers.

the whole time you were listening

to my heart,

you were thinking about how different

hers sounded.

risk

most of us only fall in love

three or four times

in our entire lives.

why waste the second time

pining for the first

when you're not even

their fourth?

Lightning Source UK Ltd.
Milton Keynes UK
UKOW01f0114070716

277862UK00002B/324/P